Snip!

'Snip!'

An original concept by Jill Atkins

© Jill Atkins 2024

Illustrated by Carissa Harris

Published by MAVERICK ARTS PUBLISHING LTD

Studio 11, City Business Centre, 6 Brighton Road,

Horsham, West Sussex, RH13 5BB

© Maverick Arts Publishing Limited May 2024

+44 (0)1403 256941

ISBN 978-1-83511-003-4

Printed in India

Maverick
publishing

www.maverickbooks.co.uk

Orange

This book is rated as: Orange Band (Guided Reading)
It follows the requirements for Phase 5 phonics.
Most words are decodable, and any non-decodable words are familiar,
supported by the context and/or represented in the artwork.

Snip!

By Jill Atkins

Illustrated by
Carissa Harris

Charlie had long hair.
Sometimes, he had it
in a ponytail...

...a top knot...

...or even bunches.

But he hated having it washed
because soap got in his eyes.

He hated having it brushed

because it was full of tangles.

"Why don't you have it trimmed a bit?"

said Mum.

Charlie frowned. "I'm frightened," he said.

"There's nothing to be afraid of," said Mum.

One day, they were walking past a barber's shop.

"Why don't we pop in here?" said Mum.

Charlie could hear scissors snipping.

He shuddered and shook his head.

The next day, Gran came to stay.

She brought her dog, Rosie, with her.

Charlie stared at Rosie.

"I can't see her eyes," laughed Charlie.

"And I can't see her nose."

In fact, he couldn't see her face at all.

It was covered in her shaggy coat.

Gran grinned.

"I need to take her to the dog grooming shop," she said. "Will you come with me?"

Charlie nodded.

When they got there, Rosie started
to shake.

"She is frightened," said Gran. "Will you help me look after her?"

"Yes," said Charlie.

Charlie sat with Rosie and put his arm around her neck.

"You'll be alright," he said. "There's nothing to be afraid of."

The grooming lady began to snip away at Rosie's shaggy coat.

Snip! Snip! Snip!

The shaggy coat fell to the ground.

Soon, Rosie looked very smart.

"She looks so cool!" laughed Charlie.

"Thank you for helping," said Gran. "She didn't mind having her coat cut at all." Charlie grinned.

BARBER SHOP

Come in
we're
Open

As they walked home, they passed the barber's shop again.

Charlie could see some boys having their hair cut.

They didn't look nervous at all.

Charlie looked up at Gran. "How about we give Mum a big surprise?" he said.

When they reached home,

Charlie rang the bell.

Mum came to the door. She looked at

Gran and Rosie. Then she looked at Charlie.

"Wow!" she said. "You've had your hair cut.

Well done for being brave!"

Charlie grinned.

"You and Rosie both look so cool!"

said Mum.

Quiz

1. Why did Charlie hate having his hair washed?
a) It took too long
b) Soap got in his eyes
c) It was boring

2. Why did Charlie not want his hair cut?
a) He was frightened
b) He wanted to grow it longer
c) He couldn't be bothered

3. What was Gran's dog called?
a) Charlie
b) Ruby
c) Rosie

4. Where did Gran and Charlie take Rosie?
a) The dog grooming shop
b) The pet shop
c) The park

5. Who got their hair cut?
a) Mum
b) Charlie and Rosie
c) Gran

Turn over for answers

Book Bands for Guided Reading

Pink

Red

Yellow

Blue

Green

Orange

Turquoise

Purple

Gold

White

The Institute of Education book banding system is a scale of colours that reflects the various levels of reading difficulty. The bands are assigned by taking into account the content, the language style, the layout and phonics. Word, phrase and sentence level work is also taken into consideration.

Maverick Early Readers are a bright, attractive range of books covering the pink to white bands. All of these books have been book banded for guided reading to the industry standard and edited by a leading educational consultant.

Cool Duck and Lots of Hats

Catch It, Jess! and Cat Nap

The Space Race

Pirates Don't Drive Diggers

A Right Royal Mess

To view the whole Maverick Readers scheme, visit our website at www.maverickearlyreaders.com

Or scan the QR code above to view our scheme instantly!

Quiz Answers: 1b, 2a, 3c, 4a, 5b